WITHDRAWN

THE BIRTHDAY OF THE INFANTA

and Other Tales

Oscar Wilde
THE BIRTHDAY
OF THE INFANTA
AND OTHER TALES

Illustrated by
BENI MONTRESOR

New York · ATHENEUM · 1982

For Ruben, a Sweet Prince

LIBRARY OF CONGRESS CATALOGING IN PUBLICATION DATA. Wilde, Oscar, 1854-1900.
The birthday of the infanta & other tales. CONTENTS: The birthday of the infanta—
The selfish giant—The nightingale & the rose—The young king—(etc.) 1. Fairy tales,
English. 2. Children's stories, English. (1. Fairy tales. 2. Short stories) I. Montresor,
Beni II. Title. PZ8.W647Bj 1981 (Fic) 81-1402. ISBN 0-689-30850-7. AACR2. Abridged text
& pictures copyright © 1982 by Beni Montresor. All rights reserved. Published simultaneously
in Canada by McCelland & Stewart, Ltd. Composition by Dix Type, Inc., Syracuse, N.Y.
Printed and bound by Mondadori, Verona, Italy. Designed by Mary Ahern & Beni Montresor.
First American Edition

C O N T E N T S

THE BIRTHDAY
OF THE INFANTA

IT was the birthday of the Infanta. She was just twelve years of age, and the sun was shining brightly in the gardens of the palace.

Although she was a real Princess and the Infanta of Spain, she had only one birthday every year, so it was naturally a matter of great importance that she should have a really fine day for the occasion. And a really fine day it certainly was. The tall striped tulips stood straight up upon their stalks, like long rows of soldiers, and looked defiantly across the grass at the roses, and said: "We are quite as splendid as you are now." The purple butterflies fluttered about with gold dust on their wings, visiting each flower in turn; the little lizards crept out of the crevices of the wall and lay basking in the white glare. And the magnolia trees opened their great globelike blossoms of folded ivory and filled the air with a sweet, heavy perfume.

The little Princess herself walked up and down the terrace with her companions and played at hide and seek round the stone vases and the old moss-grown statues. On ordinary days she was only allowed to play with children of her own rank, so she had always to play alone, but her birthday was an exception, and the King had given orders that she was to invite any of her young friends whom she liked to come and amuse themselves with her.

From a window in the palace the sad, melancholy King watched them. Behind him stood his brother, Don Pedro of Aragon, whom he hated, and his confessor, the Grand Inquisitor of Granada, sat by his side. Sadder even than usual was the King, for as he looked at the Infanta he thought of the young Queen, her mother, who had come from the gay country of France and had withered away in the somber splendor of the Spanish court, dying just six months after the birth of her child.

Certainly he had loved her madly. He had hardly ever permitted her to be out of his sight; for her, he had forgotten or seemed to have forgotten, all grave affairs of State. When she died he was, for a time, like one bereft of reason.

His whole married life seemed to come back to him today as he watched the Infanta playing on the terrace. She had all the Queen's pretty petulance of manner, the same wilful way of tossing her head, the same proud, curved, beautiful mouth, the same wonderful smile as she glanced up now and then at the window. But the shrill laughter of the children grated on his ears, and the bright pitiless sunlight mocked his sorrow. He buried his face in his hands, and when the Infanta looked up again the curtains had been drawn, and the King had retired.

She shrugged her shoulders. Surely he might have stayed with her on her birthday. What did the stupid State affairs matter? How silly of him, when the sun was shining so brightly, and everybody was so happy! Besides, he would miss the sham bull fight for which the trumpet was already sounding, to say nothing of the puppet show and the other wonderful things. Her uncle and the Grand Inquisitor were much more sensible. They had come out on the terrace and paid her nice compliments. So she tossed her pretty head, and taking Don Pedro by the hand, she walked slowly down the steps toward a long pavilion of purple silk that had been erected at the end of the garden.

A PROCESSION of noble boys came out to meet her, and the young Count of Tierra-Nueva, a wonderfully handsome lad of about fourteen years of age, led her solemnly into a little gilt and ivory chair

that was placed on a raised dais above the arena. The children grouped themselves all round, fluttering their big fans and whispering to each other, and Don Pedro and the Grand Inquisitor stood laughing at the entrance.

It certainly was a marvelous bullfight, and much nicer, the Infanta thought, than the real bullfight that she had been brought to see at Seville. Some of the boys pranced about on richly caparisoned hobbyhorses, brandishing long javelins with gay streamers of bright ribands attached to them; others went on foot, waving their scarlet cloaks before the bull and vaulting lightly over the barrier when he charged them; and as for the bull himself, he was just like a live bull, though he was only made of wickerwork and stretched

hide, and sometimes insisted on running round the arena on his hind legs, which no live bull ever dreams of doing. He made a splendid fight of it too, and the children got so excited that they stood up upon the benches and waved their lace handkerchiefs and cried out: *Bravo toro! Bravo toro!* At last, however, after a prolonged combat, during which several of the hobbyhorses were gored through and through, and their riders dismounted, the young Count of Tierra-Nueva brought the bull to his knees and, having obtained permission from the Infanta, plunged his wooden sword into the neck of the animal with such violence that the head came right off and disclosed the laughing face of little Monsieur de Lorraine, the son of the French Ambassador at Madrid.

The arena was then cleared amidst much applause, and the dead hobbyhorses dragged solemnly away and some Italian puppets appeared on the stage of a small theater that had been built up for the purpose. They acted so well, and their gestures were so extremely natural, that at the close of the play, a tragedy, the eyes of the Infanta were quite dim with tears. Indeed some of the children really cried and had to be comforted with sweetmeats.

An African juggler followed, who brought in a large flat basket covered with a red cloth, and having placed it in the center of the arena, he took from his turban a curious reed pipe and blew through it. In a few moments the cloth began to move, and as the pipe grew shriller and shriller, two green and gold snakes put out their strange wedge-shaped heads and rose slowly up, swaying to and fro with the music. The children, however, were rather frightened at their quick darting tongues and were much more pleased when the juggler made a tiny orange tree grow out of the sand and bear pretty white blossoms and clusters of real fruit; and when he took the fan of the little daughter of the Marquess de Las-Torres and changed it into a bluebird that flew all round the pavilion and sang, their delight and amazement knew no bounds. The solemn minuet, too, performed by the dancing boys from the church of Nuestra Señora Del Pilar, was charming.

A troop of handsome Egyptians — as the gypsies were termed in those days — then advanced into the arena and, sitting down cross-legs in a circle, began to play softly upon their zithers, moving their bodies to the tune

and humming, almost below their breath, a low, dreamy air, their heads beginning to nod as though they were falling asleep. Suddenly, with a cry so shrill that all the children were startled, and Don Pedro's hand clutched at the agate pommel of his dagger, they leaped to their feet and whirled madly round the enclosure beating their tambourines and chanting some wild love song. Then at another signal, they all flung themselves again to the ground and lay there quite still, the dull strumming of the zithers being the only sound that broke the silence. After that they disappeared for a moment and came back leading a brown shaggy bear by a chain and carrying on their shoulders some little Barbary apes. The bear stood upon his head with the utmost gravity, and the wizened apes played all kinds of amusing tricks with two gypsy boys who seemed to be their masters. The gypsies were a great success.

But the funniest part of the whole morning's entertainment was undoubtedly the dancing of the little Dwarf. When he stumbled into the arena, waddling on his crooked legs and wagging his huge misshapen head from side to side, the children went off into a loud shout of delight, and the Infanta herself laughed so much that Don Pedro was obliged to remind her that a Princess of the blood royal did not make so merry before those who were her inferiors in birth. The Dwarf, however, was really quite irresistible. It was his first appearance. He had been discovered only the day before, running wild through the forest by two nobles, and had been carried off by them as a surprise for the Infanta. His father, who was a poor charcoal-burner, was but too well pleased to get rid of so ugly and useless a child. Perhaps the most amusing thing about him was his complete unconsciousness of his own grotesque appearance. Indeed he seemed quite happy and full of the highest spirits. When the children laughed, he laughed as freely and as joyously as any of them, and at the close of each dance he made them each the funniest of bows, smiling and nodding at them just as if he was really one of themselves and not a little misshapen thing. As for the Infanta, she absolutely fascinated him. He could not keep his eyes off her and seemed to dance for her alone. At the close of the performance, remembering how she had seen the great ladies of the Court throw bouquets to Caffarelli, the famous Italian treble, the Infanta took out of her hair a beautiful white rose and, partly for a jest, threw

it to him across the arena with her sweetest smile. Pressing the flower to his rough, coarse lips, he put his hand upon his heart and sank on one knee before her, grinning from ear to ear.

This so upset the gravity of the Infanta that she kept on laughing long after the little Dwarf had run out of the arena and expressed a desire to her uncle that the dance should be immediately repeated. However, it was decided that it would be better for her Highness to return without delay to the Palace, where a wonderful feast had been prepared for her, including a real birthday cake with her own initials worked all over it in painted sugar and a lovely silver flag waving from the top. The Infanta accordingly rose up with

much dignity, and having given orders that the little Dwarf was to dance again for her after the hour of siesta and conveyed her thanks to the young Count of Tierra-Nueva for his charming reception, she went back to her apartments, the children following in the same order in which they had entered.

NOW when the little Dwarf heard that he was to dance a second time before the Infanta, and by her own express command, he was so proud that he ran out into the garden, kissing the white rose in an absurd ecstasy of pleasure.

The Flowers were quite indignant at his daring to intrude into their beautiful home, and when they saw him capering up and down the walks and waving his arms above his head in such a ridiculous manner, they could not restrain their feelings.

"He is really far too ugly to be allowed to play in any place where we are," cried the Tulips.

"And he has actually got one of my best blooms," exclaimed the white Rose tree. "I gave it to the Infanta this morning myself, as a birthday present, and he has stolen it from her."

As for the old Sundial, he was so taken aback by the little Dwarf's appearance that he almost forgot to mark two whole minutes with his long, shadowy finger.

But the Birds liked him. They had seen him often in the forest, dancing about like an elf after the eddying leaves, or crouched up in the hollow of some old oak tree, sharing his nuts with the squirrels. They did not mind his being ugly a bit. Besides, he had been kind to them. During that terribly bitter winter, when there were no berries on the trees and the ground was as hard as iron and the wolves had come down to the very gates of the city to look for food, he had never once forgotten them, but had always given them crumbs out of his little hunch of black bread.

So they flew round and round him, just touching his cheek with their wings as they passed, and the little Dwarf was so pleased that he could not help showing them the beautiful white rose and telling them that the Infanta herself had given it to him because she loved him.

The Lizards also took an immense fancy to him, and when he grew tired of running about and flung himself down on the grass to rest, they played and romped all over him and tried to amuse him in the best way they could.

The Flowers, however, were excessively annoyed at their behavior and at the behavior of the Birds. So they put their noses in the air and looked very haughty and were quite delighted when after some time they saw the little Dwarf scramble up from the grass and make his way across the terrace to the palace.

"He should certainly be kept indoors for the rest of his natural life," they said.

But the little Dwarf knew nothing of all this. He liked the birds and the lizards immensely and thought that the flowers were the most marvelous things in the whole world, except of course the Infanta. How he wished that he had gone back with her! She would have put him on her right hand and smiled at him, and he would have never left her side, but would have taught her all kinds of delightful tricks. For though he had never been in a palace before, he knew a great many wonderful things. He could make little cages out of rushes for the grasshoppers to sing in, and he knew the cry of every bird and could call the starlings from the treetop, or the heron from the mere. He knew the trail of every animal and would track the hare by its delicate footprints and the boar by the trampled leaves. He knew where the wood pigeons built their nests, and once when a fowler had snared the parent birds, he had brought up the young ones himself. They were quite tame and used to feed out of his hands every morning. Yes, the Infanta must certainly come to the forest and play with him. He would give her his own little bed and would watch outside the window till dawn to see that the wild, horned cattle did not harm her, nor the gaunt wolves creep too near the hut. And at dawn he would tap at the shutters and wake her, and they would go out and dance together all the day long. It was really not a bit lonely in the forest. Certainly there was a great deal to look at and when she was tired he would find a soft bank of moss for her, or carry her in his arms, for he was very strong, though he knew that he was not tall. He would make her a necklace of red briony berries, that would be quite as pretty as the white berries that she wore on her dress, and when she was tired of them, she could throw them away, and he would find her others. He would bring her acorn cups and dew-drenched anemones, and tiny glow-worms to be stars in the pale gold of her hair.

But where was she? He asked the white rose, and it made him no answer. The whole palace seemed asleep. He wandered all round looking for some place through which he might gain an entrance, and at last he caught sight of a little private door that was lying open. He slipped through and found himself in a splendid hall, far more splendid, he feared, than the forest. But the little Infanta was not there, only some wonderful white statues that looked down on him from their jasper pedestal.

At the end of the hall hung a richly embroidered curtain of black velvet, powdered with suns and stars. Perhaps she was hiding behind that? He would try at any rate.

So he stole quietly across and drew it aside. No; there was only another room, though a prettier room, he thought, than the one he had just left. The walls were hung with a many-figured green arras of needle-wrought tapestry representing a hunt.

The little Dwarf looked in wonder all round him, and was half-afraid to go on. The strange, silent horsemen that galloped so swiftly through the long glades without making any noise seemed to him like the Comprachos, who hunt only at night, and if they meet a man, turn him into a hind, and chase him. But he thought of the pretty Infanta and took courage. He wanted to find her alone and to tell her that he too loved her. Perhaps she was in the room beyond.

He ran across the soft Moorish carpets and opened the door. No? She was not here either. The room was quite empty.

It was a throne room, used for the reception of foreign ambassadors. The hangings were of gilt Cordovan leather, and a heavy gilt chandelier with branches for three hundred wax lights hung down from the black and white ceiling. Underneath a great canopy of gold cloth, on which the lions and towers of Castile were broidered in seed pearls, stood the throne itself, covered with a rich pall of black velvet studded with silver tulips and elaborately fringed with silver and pearls.

But the little Dwarf cared nothing for all this magnificence. He would not have given his rose for all the pearls on the canopy, nor one white petal of his rose for the throne itself. What he wanted was to see the Infanta and to ask her to come away with him when he had finished his dance. Here, in the Palace, the air was close and heavy, but in the forest the wind blew free and the sunlight with wandering hands of gold moved the tremulous leaves aside. There were flowers, too, in the forest, not so splendid, perhaps, as the flowers in the garden, but more sweetly scented for all that. Yes: surely she would come if he could only find her! She would come with him to the fair forest, and all day long he would dance for her delight. A smile lit up his eyes at the thought, and he passed into the next room.

Of all the rooms this was the brightest and the most beautiful. The walls were covered with a pink-flowered damask, patterned with birds and dotted with dainty blossoms of silver; the furniture was of massive silver, festooned with florid wreaths and swinging Cupids; in front of the two large fireplaces stood great screens broidered with parrots and peacocks, and the floor, which was of sea-green onyx, seemed to stretch far away into the distance. Nor was he alone. Standing under the shadow of the doorway, at the extreme end of the room, he saw a little figure watching him. His heart trembled, a cry of joy broke from his lips, and he moved out into the sunlight. As he did so, the figure moved out also, and he saw it plainly.

It was a monster, the most grotesque monster he had ever beheld. Not properly shaped as all other people were, but hunchbacked and crooked-limbed, with huge lolling head and mane of black hair. The little Dwarf frowned, and the monster frowned also. He laughed, and it laughed with him and held its hands to its sides, just as he himself was doing. He made it a mocking bow, and it returned him a low reverence. He went toward it, and it came to meet him, copying each step that he made and stopping when he stopped himself. He shouted with amusement and ran forward and reached out his hand, and the hand of the monster touched his, and it was as cold as ice. He grew afraid and moved his hand across, and the monster's hand followed it quickly. He tried to press on, but something smooth and hard stopped him. The face of the monster was now close to his own and seemed full of terror. He brushed his hair off his eyes. It imitated him. He struck at it, and it returned blow for blow. He loathed it, and it made hideous faces at him. He drew back, and it retreated.

What was it? He thought for a moment and looked round at the rest of the room. It was strange, but everything seemed to have its double in this invisible wall of clear water. Yes, picture for picture was repeated, and couch for couch.

Was it Echo? He had called to her once in the valley, and she had answered him word for word. Could she mock the eye, as she mocked the voice? Could she make a mimic world just like the real world? Could the

20

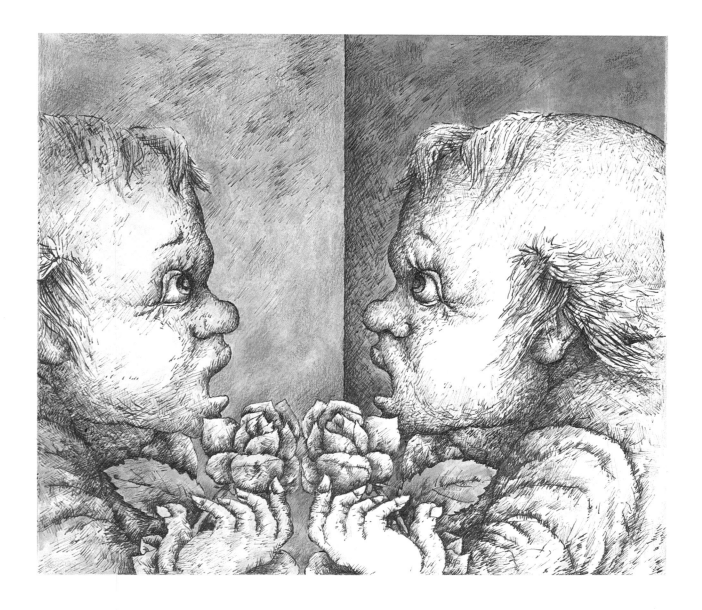

shadows of things have color and life and movement? Could it be that — ?

He started, and taking from his breast the beautiful white rose, he turned round and kissed it. The monster had a rose of its own, petal for petal the same! It kissed it with like kisses and pressed it to its heart with horrible gestures.

When the truth dawned upon him, he gave a wild cry of despair and fell sobbing to the ground. So it was he who was misshapen and hunchbacked, foul to look at and grotesque. He himself was the monster, and it was at him that all the children had been laughing, and the little Princess who he had thought loved him — she, too, had been merely mocking at his ugliness and making merry over his twisted limbs. Why had they not left him in the forest, where there was no mirror to tell him how loathsome he was? The hot tears poured down his cheeks, and he tore the white rose to pieces. The sprawling monster did the same and scattered the faint petals in the air. When he looked at it, it watched him with a face drawn with pain. He crept away, lest he should see it, and covered his eyes with his hands. He crawled, like some wounded thing, into the shadow and lay there moaning.

And at that moment the Infanta herself came in with her companions through the open window, and when they saw the ugly little dwarf lying on the ground and beating the floor with his clenched hands, in the most fantastic and exaggerated manner, they went off into shouts of happy laughter and stood all round him and watched him.

"His dancing was funny," said the Infanta; "but his acting is funnier still. Indeed, he is almost as good as the puppets, only, of course, not quite so natural."

But the little Dwarf never looked up, and his sobs grew fainter and fainter, and suddenly he gave a curious gasp and clutched his side. And then he fell back again and lay quite still.

"That is capital," said the Infanta, after a pause; "but now you must dance for me."

"Yes," cried all the children, "you must get up and dance, for you are as clever as the Barbary apes and much more ridiculous."

But the little Dwarf made no answer.

And the Infanta stamped her foot and called out to her uncle, who was walking on the terrace with the Chamberlain. "My funny little dwarf is sulking," she cried, "you must wake him up and tell him to dance for me."

They smiled at each other and sauntered in, and Don Pedro stooped down and slapped the Dwarf on the cheek with his embroidered glove. "You must dance," he said, "*petit monstre.* You must dance. The Infanta of Spain and the Indies wishes to be amused."

But the little Dwarf never moved.

"A whipping master should be sent for," said Don Pedro wearily, and he went back to the terrace. But the Chamberlain looked grave, and he

22

knelt beside the little Dwarf and put his hand upon his heart. And after a few moments he shrugged his shoulders and rose up, having made a low bow to the Infanta, he said —

"*Mi bella Princesa,* your funny little dwarf will never dance again. It is a pity, for he is so ugly that he might have made the King smile."

"But why will he not dance again?" asked the Infanta, laughing.

"Because his heart is broken," answered the Chamberlain.

And the Infanta frowned, and her dainty rose-leaf lips curled in pretty disdain. "For the future let those who come to play with me have no hearts," she cried, and she ran out into the garden.

T H E   S E L F I S H   G I A N T

EVERY afternoon, as they were coming from school, the children used to go and play in the Giant's garden.

It was a large, lovely garden, with soft green grass. Here and there over the grass stood beautiful flowers like stars, and there were twelve peach trees that in the springtime broke out into delicate blossoms of pink and pearl and in the autumn bore rich fruit. The birds sat on the trees and sang so sweetly that the children used to stop their games in order to listen to them. "How happy we are here!" they cried to each other.

One day the Giant came back. When he arrived he saw the children playing in the garden.

"What are you doing here?" he cried in a very gruff voice, and the children ran away.

"My own garden is my own garden," said the Giant; "I will allow nobody to play in it but myself." So he built a high wall all round it and put up a notice-board.

TRESPASSERS
WILL BE
PROSECUTED

The poor children had now nowhere to play. They tried to play on the road, but the road was very dusty and full of hard stones, and they did not like it.

Then the Spring came, and all over the country there were little blossoms and little birds. Only in the garden of the Selfish Giant it was still winter. The birds did not care to sing in it as there were no children, and the trees forgot to blossom. The only people who were pleased were the Snow and the Frost. "Spring has forgotten this garden," they cried, "so we will live here all the year round." The Snow covered up the grass with her great white cloak, and the Frost painted all the trees silver. Then they invited the North Wind to stay with them, and he came. He was wrapped in furs, and he roared all day about the garden.

"I cannot understand why the Spring is so late in coming," said the Selfish Giant, as he sat at the window and looked out at his cold, white garden.

But the Spring never came, nor the Summer. The Autumn gave golden fruit to every garden, but to the Giant's garden she gave none. "He is too selfish," she said. So it was always winter there.

One morning the Giant was lying awake in bed when he heard some lovely music. It sounded so sweet that he thought it must be the King's musicians passing by. It was really only a little linnet singing outside his window, but it was so long since he had heard a bird sing in his garden that it seemed to him to be the most beautiful music in the world. Then a delicious perfume came to him through the open casement. "I believe the Spring has come at last," said the Giant; and he jumped out of bed and looked out.

What did he see?

He saw a most wonderful sight. Through a little hole in the wall the children had crept in, and they were sitting in the branches of the trees. In every tree that he could see there was a little child. And the trees were so glad to have the children back again that they had covered themselves with blossoms. The birds were flying about and twittering with delight, and the flowers were looking up through the green grass and laughing. It was a lovely scene, only in one corner it was still winter. It was the farthest corner of the garden,

and in it was standing a little boy. He was so small that he could not reach up to the branches of the tree, and he was wandering all round it, crying bitterly. The poor tree was still covered with frost and snow, and the North Wind was blowing and roaring above it. "Climb up! little boy," said the Tree, and it bent its branches down as low as it could; but the boy was too tiny.

And the Giant's heart melted, as he looked out. "How selfish I have been!" he said; "now I know why the Spring would not come here. I will put that poor little boy on the top of the tree, and then I will knock down the wall, and my garden shall be the children's playground for ever and ever."

So he crept downstairs and opened the front door quite softly and

went out into the garden. But when the children saw him they were so frightened that they all ran away, and the garden became winter again. Only the little boy did not run, for his eyes were so full of tears that he did not see the Giant coming. And the Giant stole up behind him and took him gently in his hand and put him up into the tree. And the tree broke at once into blossom, and the birds came and sang on it, and the little boy stretched out his two arms and flung them round the Giant's neck and kissed him. And the other children, when they saw that the Giant was not wicked any longer, came running back. "It is your garden now, little children," said the Giant, and he took a great axe and knocked down the wall.

All day long they played, and in the evening they came to the Giant to bid him good-bye.

"But where is your little companion?" he said; "the boy I put into the tree."

"We don't know," answered the children; "he has gone away."

"You must tell him to be sure and come tomorrow," said the Giant. But the children said that they did not know where he lived and had never seen him before; and the Giant felt very sad.

Every afternoon, when school was over, the children came and played with the Giant. But the little boy whom the Giant loved was never seen again.

Years went over, and the Giant grew very old.

One winter morning he looked out of his window as he was dressing. He did not hate the Winter now, for he knew that it was merely the Spring asleep.

Suddenly he rubbed his eyes in wonder and looked and looked. In the farthest corner of the garden was a tree quite covered with lovely white blossoms. Its branches were golden, and silver fruit hung down from them, and underneath it stood the little boy he had loved.

Downstairs ran the Giant in great joy. He hastened across the grass, and came near to the child. And when he came quite close his face grew red with anger. For on the palms of the child's hands were the prints of two nails, and the prints of two nails were on the little feet.

"Who hath dared to wound thee?" cried the Giant, "tell me, that I may take my big sword and slay him."

"Nay," answered the child; "but these are the wounds of Love."

"Who art thou?" said the Giant, and a strange awe fell on him.

And the child smiled on the Giant, and said to him, "You let me play once in your garden, today you shall come with me to my garden, which is Paradise."

And when the children ran in that afternoon, they found the Giant lying dead under the tree, all covered with white blossoms.

T H E N I G H T I N G A L E
& T H E R O S E

"SHE said that she would dance with me if I brought her red roses," cried the young Student, "but in all my garden there is no red rose."

From her nest in the holm oak tree the Nightingale heard him, and she looked out through the leaves and wondered.

"No red rose in all my garden!" he cried, and his beautiful eyes filled with tears.

"Here at last is a true lover," said the Nightingale. "Passion has made his face like pale ivory and sorrow has set her seal upon his brow."

"The Prince gives a ball tomorrow night," murmured the young Student, "and my love will be of the company. If I bring her a red rose she will dance with me till dawn. But there is no red rose in my garden, so I shall sit lonely and she will pass me by."

"Here, indeed, is the true lover," said the Nightingale. "Surely love is a wonderful thing. It is more precious than emeralds and dearer than fine opals. It may not be purchased of the merchants, nor can it be weighed out in the balance for gold."

"The musicians will sit in their gallery," said the young Student, "and my love will dance to the sound of the harp and the violin. But with me she will not dance, for I have no red rose to give her," and he flung himself down on the grass and buried his face in his hands and wept.

"Why is he weeping?" asked a little Green Lizard, as he ran past him with his tail in the air.

"Why, indeed?" said a Butterfly, who was fluttering about after a sunbeam.

"He is weeping for a red rose," said the Nightingale.

"For a red rose?" they cried; "how very ridiculous!"

But the Nightingale understood the secret of the Student's sorrow, and she sat silent in the oak tree and thought about the mystery of Love.

Suddenly she spread her brown wings for flight and soared into the air.

In the center of the grass plot was standing a beautiful rose tree, and when she saw it she flew over to it and lit upon a spray.

"Give me a red rose," she cried, "and I will sing you my sweetest song."

But the Tree shook its head.

"My roses are white," it answered. "But go to my brother who grows round the old sundial, and perhaps he will give you what you want."

So the Nightingale flew over to the Rose tree that was growing round the old sundial.

"Give me a red rose," she cried, "and I will sing you my sweetest song."

But the Tree shook its head.

"My roses are yellow," it answered. "But go to my brother who grows beneath the Student's window, and perhaps he will give you what you want."

So the Nightingale flew over to the Rose tree that was growing beneath the Student's window.

"Give me a red rose," she cried, "and I will sing you my sweetest song."

But the Tree shook its head.

"My roses are red," it answered. "But the winter has chilled my veins, and the frost has nipped my buds, and I shall have no roses at all this year."

"One red rose is all I want," cried the Nightingale, "only one red rose! Is there no way by which I can get it?"

"There is a way," answered the Tree; "but it is so terrible that I dare not tell it to you."

"Tell it to me," said the Nightingale. "I am not afraid."

"If you want a red rose," said the Tree, "you must build it out of

music by moonlight, and stain it with your own heart's-blood. You must sing to me with your breast against a thorn. All night long you must sing to me, and the thorn must pierce your heart, and your life-blood must flow into my veins and become mine."

"Death is a great price to pay for a red rose," cried the Nightingale, "and Life is very dear to all. Yet Love is better than Life, and what is the heart of a bird compared to the heart of a man?"

So she spread her brown wings for flight and soared into the air.

The young Student was still lying on the grass and the tears were not yet dry in his beautiful eyes.

"Be happy," cried the Nightingale, "be happy; you shall have your red rose."

The Student looked up from the grass and listened, but he could not understand what the Nightingale was saying to him, for he only knew the things that are written down in books.

But the Oak tree understood and felt sad, for he was very fond of the little Nightingale who had built her nest in his branches.

"Sing me one last song," he whispered; "I shall feel lonely when you are gone."

So the Nightingale sang to the Oak tree, and her voice was like water bubbling from a silver jar.

When she had finished her song, the Student got up, and he went into his room and lay down on his little pallet-bed and began to think of his love; and, after a time, he fell asleep.

And when the moon shone in the heavens the Nightingale flew to the Rose tree and set her breast against the thorn. All night long she sang, with her breast against the thorn. All night long she sang, and the thorn went deeper and deeper into her breast, and her life-blood ebbed away from her.

And on the topmost spray of the Rose tree there blossomed a marvelous rose, petal following petal, as song followed song. Pale was it, at first, but the tree cried to the Nightingale to press closer against the thorn. "Press closer, little Nightingale," cried the Tree, "or the Day will come before the rose is finished."

So the Nightingale pressed closer against the thorn and louder and louder grew her song. And a delicate flush of pink came into the leaves of the rose. But the thorn had not yet reached her heart, so the rose's heart remained white.

And the Tree cried to the Nightingale to press closer against the thorn. "Press closer, little Nightingale," cried the Tree, "or the Day will come before the rose is finished."

So the Nightingale pressed closer against the thorn, and the thorn touched her heart, and a fierce pang of pain shot through her. Bitter, bitter was the pain, and wilder and wilder grew her song.

And the marvelous rose became crimson, like the rose of the eastern sky. Crimson was the girdle of petals, and crimson as a ruby was the heart.

But the Nightingale's voice grew fainter, and her little wings began to beat, and a film came over her eyes.

The she gave one last burst of music. The red rose heard it, and it trembled all over with ecstasy and opened its petals to the cold morning air.

"Look, look!" cried the Tree, "the rose is finished now"; but the Nightingale made no answer, for she was lying dead in the long grass, with the thorn in her heart.

And at noon the Student opened his window and looked out.

"Why, what a wonderful piece of luck!" he cried; "here is a red rose! I have never seen any rose like it in all my life." And he leaned down and plucked it.

Then he put on his hat and ran up to the Professor's house with the rose in his hand.

The daughter of the Professor was sitting in the doorway winding blue silk on a reel.

"You said that you would dance with me if I brought you a red rose," cried the Student. "Here is the reddest rose in all the world."

But the girl frowned.

"I am afraid it will not go with my dress," she answered; "and, besides, the Chamberlain's nephew has sent me some real jewels, and everybody knows that jewels cost far more than flowers."

40

"Well, upon my word, you are very ungrateful," said the Student angrily; and he threw the rose into the street, where it fell into the gutter, and a cart wheel went over it.

"Ungrateful!" said the girl. "I tell you what, you are very rude; and, after all, who are you? Only a Student." And she got up from her chair and went into the house.

"What a silly thing Love is!" said the Student as he walked away. "It is not half as useful as Logic, for it does not prove anything, and it is always telling one of things that are not going to happen and making one believe things that are not true. I shall go back to Philosophy and study Metaphysics."

So he returned to his room and pulled out a great dusty book and began to read.

T H E   Y O U N G   K I N G

IT was the night before the day fixed for his coronation, and the young King was sitting alone in his beautiful chamber. The lad — for he was only a lad — had flung himself back with a deep sigh of relief on the soft cushions of his embroidered couch, lying there, wild-eyed and open-mouthed, like some young animal of the forest newly snared by the hunters.

And, indeed, it was the hunters who had found him, coming upon him almost by chance as he was following the flock of the poor goatherd who had brought him up, and whose son he had always fancied himself to be. The child of the old King's only daughter, by a secret marriage with one much beneath her in station, he had been, when but a week old, stolen away from his mother's side as she slept, and given into the charge of a common peasant and his wife, who lived in a remote part of the forest. Grief, or, as some suggested, a swift Italian poison administered in a cup of spiced wine, slew, within an hour of her wakening, the girl who had given him birth, and as the trusty messenger who bore the child across his saddle-bow stooped from his weary horse and knocked at the rude door of the goatherd's hut, the body of the Princess was being lowered into an open grave that had been dug in a deserted churchyard.

Such, at least, was the story that men whispered to each other. Certain it was that the old King, when on his death-bed, had had the lad sent for, and, in the presence of the Council, had acknowledged him as his heir.

And it seems that from the very first moment of his recognition he had shown signs of that strange passion for beauty that was destined to have so great an influence over his life. Those who accompanied him to the suite of rooms set apart for his service often spoke of the cry of pleasure that broke from his lips when he saw the delicate raiment and rich jewels that had been prepared for him, and of the almost fierce joy with which he flung aside his rough leathern tunic and coarse sheepskin cloak.

MANY curious stories were related about him. It was said that on one occasion he had been missed for several hours, and after a lengthened search had been discovered in a little chamber in one of the northern turrets of the palace gazing, as one in a trance, at a Greek gem carved with the figure of Adonis. He had been seen, so the tale ran, pressing his warm lips to the marble brow of an antique statue that had been discovered in the bed of the river. He had passed a whole night in noting the effect of the moonlight on a silver image of Endymion.

All rare and costly materials had a great fascination for him, and in his eagerness to procure them he had sent away many merchants, some to traffic for amber with the rough fisher-folk of the north seas, some to Egypt to look for that curious green turquoise which is found only in the tombs of kings, some to Persia for silken carpets and painted pottery, and others to India to buy gauze and stained ivory, moonstones and bracelets of jade, sandalwood and blue enamel.

But what had occupied him most was the robe he was to wear at his coronation, the robe of tissued gold, and the ruby-studded crown, and the scepter with its rows and rings of pearls. Indeed, it was of this that he was thinking tonight, as he lay back on his luxurious couch, watching the great pinewood log that was burning itself out on the open hearth.

After some time he rose from his seat, and leaning against the carved penthouse of the chimney, looked round at the dimly lit room. Far away, in an orchard, a nightingale was singing. A faint perfume of jasmine came through the open window. He brushed his brown curls back from his forehead and, taking up a lute, let his fingers stray across the cords. His heavy eyelids drooped, and a strange languor came over him. Never before had he felt so keenly, or with such exquisite joy, the magic and mystery of beautiful things.

When midnight sounded from the clock tower he touched a bell, and his pages entered and disrobed him with much ceremony, pouring rose-water over his hands and strewing flowers on his pillow. A few moments after that they had left the room, he fell asleep.

AND as he slept he dreamed a dream, and this was his dream. He thought that he was standing in a long, low attic, amidst the whir and clatter of many looms. The meager daylight peered in through the grated windows and showed him the gaunt figures of the weavers bending over their cases. Their faces were pinched with famine, and their thin hands shook and trembled. Some haggard women were seated at a table sewing. A horrible odor filled the place, and the walls dripped and streamed with damp.

The young King went over to one of the weavers and watched him.

And the weaver looked at him angrily and said, "Art thou a spy set on us by our master?"

"Who is thy master?" asked the young King.

"Our master!" cried the weaver bitterly. "He is a man like myself. Indeed, there is but this difference between us — that he wears fine clothes while I go in rags, and that while I am weak from hunger he suffers from overfeeding."

"The land is free," said the young King, "and thou art no man's slave."

"In war," answered the weaver, "the strong make slaves of the weak, and in peace the rich make slaves of the poor. We must work to live, and they give us such mean wages that we die. We have chains, though no eye beholds them; and we are slaves, though men call us free."

"Is it so with all?" he asked.

"It is so with all," answered the weaver, "with the young as well as with the old, with the women as well as with the men. Misery wakes us in the morning, and Shame sits with us at night. But what are these things to thee? Thou art not one of us. Thy face is too happy." And he turned away scowling and threw the shuttle across the loom, and the young King saw that it was threaded with a thread of gold.

And a great terror seized upon him, and he said to the weaver, "What robe is this that thou art weaving?"

"It is the robe for the coronation of the young King," he answered; "what is that to thee?"

And the young King gave a loud cry and woke, and lo! he was in his own chamber, and through the window he saw the great honey-colored moon hanging in the dusky air.

AND he fell asleep again, and dreamed, and this was his dream. He thought that he was lying on the deck of a huge galley that was being rowed by a hundred slaves. On a carpet by his side the master of the galley was seated.

The slaves were naked, but for a ragged loincloth, and each man was chained to his neighbor. They stretched out their lean arms and pulled the heavy cars through the water. The salt spray flew from the blades.

At last they reached a little bay and began to take soundings. As soon as they had cast anchor and hauled down the sail, men went into the hold and brought up a long rope ladder, heavily weighted with lead. The master of the galley threw it over the side, making the ends fast to two iron stanchions. Then the men seized the youngest of the slaves and filled his nostrils and ears with wax and tied a big stone round his waist. He crept wearily down the ladder and disappeared into the sea. At the prow of the galley sat a shark-charmer beating monotonously upon a drum.

After some time the diver rose up out of the water and clung panting to the ladder with a pearl in his right hand. The men seized it from him and thrust him back.

Again and again he came up, and each time that he did so he brought with him a beautiful pearl. The master of the galley weighed them and put them into a little bag of green leather.

The young King tried to speak, but his tongue seemed to cleave to the roof of his mouth, and his lips refused to move.

Then the diver came up for the last time, and the pearl that he brought with him was shaped like the full moon and whiter than the morning star. But his face was strangely pale, and as he fell upon the desk, blood gushed from his ears and nostrils. He quivered for a little, and then he was still.

And the master of the galley laughed, and reaching out, he took the pearl, and when he saw it he pressed it to his forehead and bowed. "It shall be," he said, "for the scepter of the young King."

And when the young King heard this he gave a great cry and woke, and through the window he saw the long gray fingers of dawn clutching at the fading stars.

AND he fell asleep again, and dreamed, and this was his dream. He thought that he was wandering through a dim wood, hung with strange fruits and with beautiful poisonous flowers. The adders hissed at him as he went by, and the bright parrots flew screaming from branch to branch.

On and on he went, till he reached the outskirts of the wood, and there he saw an immense multitude of men toiling in the bed of a dried-up river. They swarmed up the crag like ants. They dug deep pits in the ground and went down into them. Some of them cleft the rocks with great axes; others grabbled in the sand. They tore up the cactus by its roots and trampled on the scarlet blossoms.

From the darkness of a cavern Death and Avarice watched them, and Death said, "I am weary; give me a third of them and let me go."

But Avarice shook her head. "They are my servants," she answered.

And Death said to her, "What hast thou got in thy hand?"

"I have three grains of corn," she answered; "what is that to thee?"

"Give me one of them," cried Death, "to plant in my garden; only one of them, and I will go away."

"I will not give thee anything," said Avarice.

And Death laughed and took a cup and dipped it into a pool of water, and out of the cup rose Ague. She passed through the great multitude, and a third of them lay dead.

And when Avarice saw that a third of the multitude was dead she beat her breast and wept. "Thou hast slain a third of my servants," she cried. "Get thee gone. Get thee gone, and come here no more."

"Nay," answered Death, "but till thou has given me a grain of corn I will not go."

But Avarice shut her hand and clenched her teeth. "I will not give thee anything," she muttered.

And Death laughed and took up a black stone and threw it into the forest, and out came Fever in a robe of flame. She passed through the multitude and touched them, and each man that she touched died.

And Avarice shuddered and put ashes on her head. "Thou art cruel," she cried; "thou art cruel. Get thee gone and leave me my servants."

"Nay," answered Death, "but till thou has given me a grain of corn I will not go."

"I will not give thee anything," said Avarice.

And Death laughed again, and he whistled through his fingers, and a woman came flying through the air. Plague was written upon her forehead, and a crowd of lean vultures wheeled round her. She covered the valley with her wings, and no man was left alive.

And Avarice fled shrieking through the forest, and Death leaped upon his red horse and galloped away, and his galloping was faster than the wind.

And the young King wept, and said: "Who were these men, and for what were they seeking?"

"For rubies for a king's crown," answered one who stood behind him.

And the young King turned and saw a man habited as a pilgrim and holding in his hand a mirror of silver.

And he grew pale, and said: "For what king?"

And the pilgrim answered: "Look in this mirror, and thou shalt see him."

And he looked in the mirror, and seeing his own face, he gave a great cry and woke, and the bright sunlight was streaming into the room, and from the trees of the garden the birds were singing.

AND the Chamberlain and the high officers of State came in and made obeisance to him, and the pages brought him the robe of tissued gold and set the crown and the scepter before him.

And the young King looked at them, and they were beautiful. But he remembered his dreams, and he said to his lords: "Take these things away, for I will not wear them."

And the courtiers were amazed, and some of them laughed, for they thought that he was jesting.

But he spake sternly to them again, and said: "Take these things away and hide them from me. Though it be the day of my coronation, I will not wear them. For on the loom of sorrow and by the white hands of Pain has this my robe been woven. There is Blood in the heart of the ruby, and Death in the heart of the pearl." And he told them of his three dreams.

And the Chamberlain spake to the young King and said, "My lord, I pray thee set aside these black thoughts and put on this fair robe and set this crown upon thy head. For how shall the people know that thou art a king, if thou hast not a king's raiment?"

And the young King looked at him. "Is it so, indeed?" he questioned. "Will they not know me for a king if I have not a king's raiment?"

"They will not know thee, my lord," cried the Chamberlain.

"It may be as thou sayest. And yet I will not wear this robe, nor will I be crowned with this crown, but even as I came to the palace so will I go forth from it."

And he bade them all leave him, save one page whom he kept as his companion, and when he had bathed himself in clear water, he opened a great painted chest, and from it he took the leathern tunic and rough sheepskin cloak that he had worn when he had watched the shaggy goats of the goatherd. These he put on, and in his hand he took his rude shepherd's staff.

And the little page opened his eyes in wonder, and said, "My lord, I see thy robe and thy scepter, but where is thy crown?"

And the young King plucked a spray of wild briar that was climbing over the balcony and bent it and made a circlet of it and set it on his own head.

"This shall be my crown," he answered.

And thus attired he passed out of his chamber into the Great Hall, where the nobles were waiting for him.

And the nobles made merry, and some of them cried out to him, "My lord, the people wait for their king, and thou showest them a beggar," and others were wroth and said, "He brings shame upon our state and is unworthy to be our master." But he answered them not a word, but went down the staircase and out through the gates and mounted upon his horse and rode towards the cathedral.

And the people laughed and said, "It is the King's fool who is riding by," and they mocked him.

And he drew rein and said, "Nay, but I am the King." And he told them his three dreams.

And a man came out of the crowd and spake bitterly to him, and said, "Sir, knowest thou not that out of the luxury of the rich cometh the life of the poor? By your pomp we are nurtured, and your vices give us bread. To toil for a master is bitter, but to have no master to toil for is more bitter still."

And the young King's eyes filled with tears, and he rode on through the murmurs of the people.

And when he reached the great portal of the cathedral, the soldiers thrust their halberts out and said, "What dost thou seek here? None enters by this door but the King."

And his face flushed with anger, and he said to them, "I am the King," and waved their halberts aside and passed in.

And when the old bishop saw him coming in his goatherd's dress, he rose up in wonder from his throne and went to meet him, and said to him, "My son, is this a king's apparel? And with what crown shall I crown thee, and what scepter shall I place in thy hand? Surely this should be to thee a day of joy, and not a day of abasement."

"Shall Joy wear what Grief has fashioned?" said the young King. And he told him his three dreams.

And when the Bishop had heard them he knit his brows and said, "My son, I am an old man, and in the winter of my days, and I know that many evil things are done in the wide world. Canst thou make these things not to be? Is not He who made misery wiser than thou art? Wherefore I bid thee ride back to the Palace and make thy face glad and put on the raiment

that beseemeth a king, and with the crown of gold I will crown thee, and the scepter of pearl will I place in thy hand. And as for thy dreams, think no more of them."

"Sayest thou that in this house?" said the young King, and he strode past the Bishop and climbed up the steps of the altar. He knelt before the image of Christ and bowed his head in prayer, and the priests in their stiff copes crept away from the altar.

And suddenly a wild tumult came from the street outside, and in entered the nobles with drawn swords. "Where is this dreamer of dreams?" they cried. "Where is this King, who is apparelled like a beggar? Surely we will slay him, for he is unworthy to rule over us."

And the young King bowed his head again and prayed, and when he had finished his prayer he rose up, and turning round, he looked at them sadly.

And lo! through the painted windows came the sunlight streaming upon him, and the sunbeams wove round him a tissued robe that was fairer than the robe that had been fashioned for his pleasure. The dead staff blossomed and bore lilies that were whiter than pearls. The dry thorn blossomed, and bore roses that were redder than rubies. In the fair raiment of a king he stood before them, and the organ pealed out its music, and the trumpeters blew upon their trumpets, and the singing boys sang.

And the people fell upon their knees in awe, and the nobles sheathed their swords and did homage, and the Bishop's face grew pale, and his hands trembled. "A greater than I hath crowned thee," he cried, and he knelt before him.

And the young King came down from the high altar and passed home through the midst of the people. But no man dared look upon his face, for it was like the face of an angel.

THE HAPPY PRINCE

HIGH above the city, on a tall column, stood the statue of the Happy Prince. He was gilded all over with thin leaves of fine gold, for eyes he had two bright sapphires, and a large red ruby glowed on his sword-hilt.

He was very much admired indeed. "He is as beautiful as a weathercock," remarked one of the Town Councillors.

"Why can't you be like the Happy Prince?" asked a sensible mother of her little boy who was crying for the moon. "The Happy Prince never dreams of crying for anything."

"He looks just like an angel," said the Charity Children as they came out of the cathedral in their bright scarlet cloaks and their clean white pinafores.

"How do you know?" said the Mathematical Master; "you have never seen one."

"Ah! but we have, in our dreams," answered the children.

One night there flew over the city a little Swallow. His friends had gone away to Egypt six weeks before, but he had stayed behind, for he was in love with the most beautiful Reed.

After they had gone he felt lonely and began to tire of his lady-love. "I admit that she is domestic," he said, "but I love travelling, and my wife, consequently, should love travelling also."

"Will you come away with me?" he said finally to her, but the Reed shook her head.

"You have been trifling with me," he cried. "I am off to the Pyramids. Good-bye!" and he flew away.

All day long he flew, and at nighttime he arrived at the city. "Where shall I put up?" he said.

Then he saw the statue on the tall column.

"I will put up there," he cried. So he alighted just between the feet of the Happy Prince.

"I have a golden bedroom," he said softly to himself as he looked round, and he prepared to go to sleep; but just as he was putting his head under his wing a large drop of water fell on him. "What a curious thing!" he cried; "there is not a single cloud in the sky, and yet it is raining."

Then another drop fell.

"What is the use of a statue if it cannot keep the rain off?" he said; "I must look for a good chimney pot," and he determined to fly away.

But before he had opened his wings, a third drop fell, and he looked up.

The eyes of the Happy Prince were filled with tears, and tears were running down his golden cheeks.

"Who are you?" he said.

"I am the Happy Prince."

"Why are you weeping then?" asked the Swallow.

"When I was alive and had a human heart," answered the statue, "I did not know what tears were, for I lived in the Palace of Sans-Souci, where sorrow is not allowed to enter. My courtiers called me the Happy Prince. So I lived, and so I died. And now that I am dead they have set me up here so high that I can see all the ugliness and all the misery of my city, and though my heart is made of lead, yet I cannot choose but weep."

"Far away," continued the statue in a low musical voice, "far away in

a little street there is a poor house. One of the windows is open, and through it I can see a woman seated at a table. She is embroidering passion-flowers on a satin gown for the loveliest of the Queen's maids-of-honor to wear at the next Court ball. In a bed in the corner of the room her little boy is lying ill. He has a fever and is asking for oranges. His mother has nothing to give him but river water, so he is crying. Swallow, Swallow, little Swallow, will you not bring her the ruby out of my sword-hilt? My feet are fastened to this pedestal and I cannot move."

"I am waited for in Egypt," said the Swallow. "My friends are flying up and down the Nile and talking to the large lotus-flowers."

"Swallow, Swallow, little Swallow," said the Prince, "will you not stay with me for one night and be my messenger? The boy is so thirsty, and the mother so sad."

"I don't think I like boys," answered the Swallow. "Last summer, when I was staying on the river, there were two rude boys, the miller's sons, who were always throwing stones at me."

But the Happy Prince looked so sad that the little Swallow was sorry. "It is very cold here," he said; "but I will stay with you for one night and be your messenger."

"Thank you, little Swallow," said the Prince.

So the Swallow picked out the great ruby from the Prince's sword and flew away with it in his beak over the roofs of the town.

He passed by the cathedral tower, where the white marble angels were sculptured. He passed by the palace and a beautiful girl came out on the balcony with her lover. "How wonderful the stars are," he said to her.

"I hope my dress will be ready in time for the State ball," she answered; "I have ordered passion-flowers to be embroidered on it, but the seamstresses are so lazy."

He passed over the river, and at last he came to the poor house and looked in. The boy was tossing feverishly on his bed, and the mother had fallen asleep, she was so tired. In he hopped and laid the great ruby on the table beside the woman's thimble. Then he flew gently round the bed, fanning the boy's forehead with his wings. "How cool I feel!" said the boy, "I must be getting better."

Then the Swallow flew back to the Happy Prince and told him what he had done. "It is curious," he remarked, "but I feel quite warm now, although it is so cold."

"That is because you have done a good action," said the Prince. And the little Swallow began to think, and then he fell asleep. Thinking always made him sleepy.

When day broke he flew down to the river and had a bath. "Tonight I go to Egypt," and he was in high spirits at the prospect. He visited all the public monuments and sat a long time on top of the church steeple.

When the moon rose he flew back to the Happy Prince. "Have you

any commissions for Egypt?" he cried; "I am just starting."

"Swallow, Swallow, little Swallow," said the Prince, "will you not stay with me one night longer?"

"I am waited for in Egypt," answered the Swallow.

"Swallow, Swallow, little Swallow," said the Prince, "far away across the city I see a young man in a garret. He is leaning over a desk covered with papers. He is trying to finish a play for the Director of the Theater, but he is too cold to write any more. There is no fire in the grate, and hunger has made him faint."

"I will wait with you one night longer," said the Swallow, who really had a good heart. "Shall I take him another ruby?"

"Alas! I have no ruby now," said the Prince; "my eyes are all that I have left. They are made of rare sapphires. Pluck out one of them and take it to him. He will sell it to the jeweler and buy firewood and finish his play."

"Dear Prince," said the Swallow, "I cannot do that"; and he began to weep.

"Swallow, Swallow, little Swallow," said the Prince, "do as I command you."

So the Swallow plucked out the Prince's eye and flew away to the student's garret. It was easy enough to get in, as there was a hole in the roof. Through this he darted and came into the room. The young man had his head buried in his hands, so he did not hear the flutter of the bird's wings, and when he looked up he found the beautiful sapphire lying on the desk.

"I am beginning to be appreciated," he cried; "this is from some great admirer. Now I can finish my play," and he looked quite happy.

The next day the Swallow flew down to the harbor. He sat on the mast of a large vessel and watched the sailors hauling big chests out of the hold with ropes. And when the moon rose he flew back to the Happy Prince.

"I am come to bid you good-bye," he cried.

"Swallow, Swallow, little Swallow," said the Prince, "will you not stay with me one night longer?"

"It is winter," answered the Swallow, "and the chill snow will soon be here. In Egypt the sun is warm on the green palm trees, and the crocodiles

lie in the mud and look lazily about them."

"In the square below," said the Happy Prince, "there stands a little match-girl. She has let her matches fall in the gutter, and they are all spoiled. Her father will beat her if she does not bring home some money, and she is crying. Pluck out my other eye and give it to her, and her father will not beat her."

"I will stay with you one night longer," said the Swallow, "but I cannot pluck out your eye. You would be quite blind then."

"Swallow, Swallow, little Swallow," said the Prince, "do as I command you."

So he plucked out the Prince's other eye and darted down with it. He swooped past the match-girl and slipped the jewel into the palm of her hand. "What a lovely bit of glass!" cried the little girl; and she ran home, laughing.

Then the Swallow came back to the Prince. "You are blind now," he said, "so I will stay with you always."

"No, little Swallow," said the poor Prince, "you must go away to Egypt."

"I will stay with you always," said the Swallow, and he slept at the Prince's feet.

All the next day he sat on the Prince's shoulder and told him stories of what he had seen in strange lands. He told him of the red ibises, who stand in long rows on the banks of the Nile; of the Sphinx, who is as old as the world itself and lives in the desert; of the merchants, who walk slowly by the side of their camels and carry amber beads in their hands.

"Dear little Swallow," said the Prince, "you tell me of marvelous things, but more marvelous than anything is the suffering of men and of women. Fly over my city, little Swallow, and tell me what you see there."

So the Swallow flew over the great city and saw the rich making merry in their beautiful houses, while the beggars were sitting at the gates. He flew into dark lanes and saw the white faces of starving children looking out listlessly at the black streets.

Then he flew back and told the Prince what he had seen.

"I am covered with fine gold," said the Prince. "You must take it off, leaf by leaf, and give it to my poor."

Leaf after leaf of the fine gold the Swallow picked off, till the Happy Prince looked quite dull and gray. Leaf after leaf of the fine gold he brought to the poor, and the children's faces grew rosier, and they laughed and played games in the street. "We have bread now!" they cried.

Then the snow came, and after the snow came the frost. The poor little Swallow grew colder and colder, but he would not leave the Prince. He picked up crumbs outside the baker's door when the baker was not looking and tried to keep himself warm by flapping his wings.

But at last he knew that he was going to die. He had just enough strength to fly up to the Prince's shoulder once more. "Good-bye, dear Prince!" he murmured. "Will you let me kiss your hand?"

"I am glad that you are going to Egypt at last, little Swallow," said the Prince. "You have stayed too long here; but you must kiss me on the lips, for I love you."

"It is not to Egypt that I am going," said the Swallow. "I am going to the House of Death."

And he kissed the Happy Prince on the lips and fell down dead at his feet.

At that moment a curious crack sounded inside the statue, as if something had broken. The fact is that the leaden heart had snapped right in two.

Early the next morning the Mayor was walking in the square below in company with the Town Councillors. As they passed the column he looked up at the statue: "Dear me! how shabby the Happy Prince looks!" he said.

"How shabby, indeed!" cried the Town Councillors.

"And here is actually a dead bird at his feet!" continued the Mayor. "We must really issue a proclamation that birds are not to be allowed to die here." And the Town Clerk made a note of the suggestion.

So they pulled down the statue of the Happy Prince. "As he is no longer beautiful he is no longer useful," said the Art Professor at the University.

Then they melted the statue in a furnace.

"What a strange thing!" said the overseer of the workmen at the foundry. "This broken lead heart will not melt in the furnace. We must throw it away." So they threw it on a dust heap where the dead Swallow was also lying.

"Bring me the two most precious things in the city," said God to one of His Angels; and the Angel brought Him the leaden heart and the dead bird.

"You have rightly chosen," said God, "for in my garden of Paradise this little bird shall sing for evermore, and in my city of gold the Happy Prince shall praise me."

OSCAR WILDE, the Irish-born author, playwright and wit, published these stories in 1888, and they marked the beginning of the period of his greatest creativity. Soon after came Wilde's novel, *The Picture of Dorian Gray*. Then between 1892 and 1895 Wilde wrote four plays, including *Lady Windermere's Fan* and *The Importance of Being Earnest*, both of which are still performed. He died in Paris in 1900.

BENI MONTRESOR won the Caldecott Medal for the best picture book of the year for *May I Bring a Friend*. Illustrator, author, film director, theater designer, his sets and costumes can be seen at all of the major opera houses of the world, such as La Scala of Milan, The Metropolitan Opera in New York, The Royal Opera House of London and the Paris Opera.

To celebrate his twenty years in opera, The Museum of the Performing Arts of Lincoln Center in New York, in 1981, held an exhibition called *The Magic of Montresor*.

Mr. Montresor has also won the Leonide Massine Prize for ballet design and numerous awards from the Society of Illustrators. One of the films he directed, *Pilgrimage*, was selected for the Cannes Film Festival. In June of 1983, a full-length ballet version of "The Birthday of the Infanta," with music by Rimski-Korsakov and scenario by Beni Montresor, will premiere at the Teatro Regio in Turin.

Beni Montresor was born in Verona, Italy, and grew up in Venice. In 1980 he was knighted by the Italian Government for his contribution to the arts.